This book belongs to,

____

Letters written by,

____